Poppy Cotton is an ordinary girl
who lives in a pretty little cottage with
her mum and dad and the baby twins,
Angel and Archie. When she is good
everybody calls her Princess Poppy.
Her grandpa says that every
little girl is a princess, especially
when she is kind and helpful.
Are you kind and helpful too?

Honeypot Hill

Can you find the places that Poppy visits in this story?

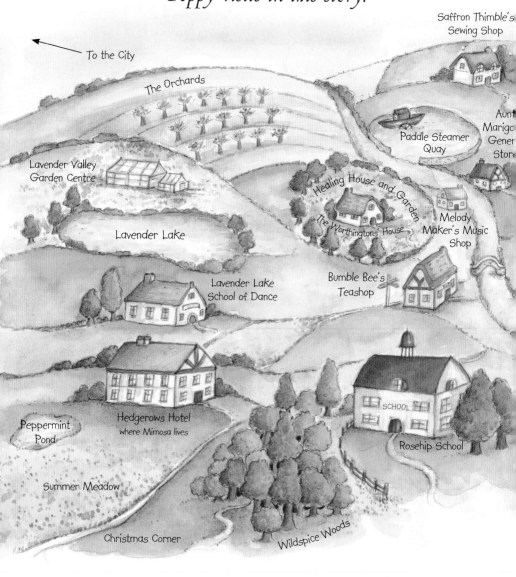

Saffron Thimble's Sewing Shop

To the City

The Orchards

Paddle Steamer Quay

Aunt Marigo Gener Store

Lavender Valley Garden Centre

Healing House and Garden

The Worthingtons' House

Melody Maker's Music Shop

Lavender Lake

Lavender Lake School of Dance

Bumble Bee's Teashop

SCHOOL

Peppermint Pond

Hedgerows Hotel
where Mimosa lives

Rosehip School

Summer Meadow

Christmas Corner

Wildspice Woods

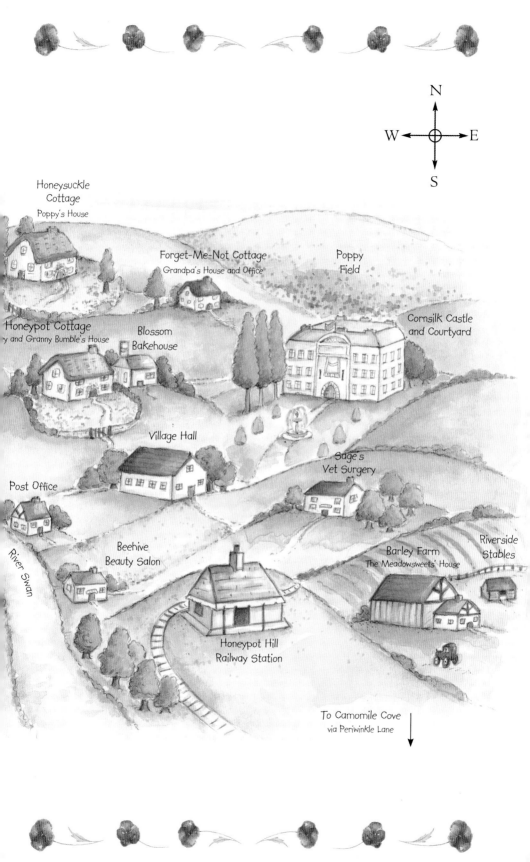

N
W ⊕ E
S

Honeysuckle Cottage
Poppy's House

Forget-Me-Not Cottage
Grandpa's House and Office

Poppy Field

Honeypot Cottage
y and Granny Bumble's House

Blossom Bakehouse

Cornsilk Castle and Courtyard

Village Hall

Sage's Vet Surgery

Post Office

Beehive Beauty Salon

Riverside Stables

Barley Farm
The Meadowsweets' House

River Swan

Honeypot Hill Railway Station

To Camomile Cove
via Periwinkle Lane

Visit Princess Poppy for fun, games,
puzzles, activities and lots more at
www.princesspoppy.com

THE PLAY
A RED FOX BOOK 978 0 552 57037 4

First published in Great Britain by Picture Corgi,
an imprint of Random House Children's Publishers UK
A Random House Group Company

This Red Fox edition published in 2013

1 3 5 7 9 10 8 6 4 2

Text copyright © Janey Louise Jones, 2006
Illustrations copyright © Picture Corgi Books, 2006
Illustrations by Veronica Vasylenko

The right of Janey Louise Jones and Veronica Vasylenko to be identified as the author and illustrator
of this work has been asserted in accordance with the Copyright, Designs and Patents Act 1988.

Red Fox Books are published by Random House Children's Publishers UK,
61–63 Uxbridge Road, London W5 5SA

www.**randomhousechildrens**.co.uk
www.**randomhouse**.co.uk
www.princesspoppy.com
Addresses for companies within The Random House Group Limited can be found at:
www.randomhouse.co.uk/offices.htm
THE RANDOM HOUSE GROUP Limited Reg. No. 954009
A CIP catalogue record for this book is available from the British Library.

Printed in China

The Play

Written by Janey Louise Jones

RED FOX

For Ben, Ollie and Louis,
with maternal and eternal love

The Play

featuring

Mum
★

Princess Poppy

Honey
★

Daisy
★

Edward
★

Grandpa
★

"Mum, I'm bored," said Poppy.

"Daisy, Edward and Grandpa will be here soon. And here comes Honey," said Mum as Poppy's best friend skipped towards them. "Maybe she will be able to think of something to do."

"Hi, Poppy," called Honey. "What are you doing?"

"Nothing," said Poppy. "My cousins are coming over with Grandpa today, but there's nothing to do. Can *you* think of anything?"

Honey sat down next to Poppy and tried to think of something to do.

"Let's put on a play," said Honey after a few minutes. "Granny Bumble took me to see one last summer. It was amazing!"

"Oooooh, that is a brilliant idea, Honey.
I have always wanted to be in a play," said
Poppy. "We are going to need

tickets,

costumes,

actors

and a story!"

"Hi, everyone!" said Poppy, as Grandpa and her cousins arrived. "Guess what we are doing today?"

Before they even had a chance to reply, Poppy started telling them about the play.

"There is so much to do. We need to start right now," she told them.

"What is the play about?" asked Grandpa.

"I'm not quite sure yet," said Poppy. "I thought *you* might be able to help us make up a story. It *has* to be about princesses. Edward can be my page boy."

"But I want to be a wizard or a pirate!" said Edward.

"Well you can't," said Poppy. "It's *my* play!"

"Stop arguing and leave it to me!" said Grandpa.

"Edward, you clear all my toys away," said
Poppy. "You make the tickets, Honey, and
hand them out to everyone in Honeypot
Hill. And Daisy, you can go and get the
dressing-up chest and make-up box from
my room."

They all sprang into action,
except Poppy.

She put on her sun-hat, sat down in her deckchair and watched the others at work. Poppy was so excited about the play, she just wanted to make sure that everything was perfect!

"Edward, you have to move *everything*,"
called Poppy.

The others looked up from what they
were doing.

"Do it yourself, Princess Bossy Boots!"
said Edward.

"Poppy, you are giving us an awful lot
of orders," said Daisy.

"And you're not doing anything,"
said Honey.

"That's not true. I am organizing the whole play," said Poppy. "It is my garden, so it is my play, and you have to do what I say."

"This isn't fun anymore," said Honey. "I'm going home."

"Let's do the play in Honey's garden," said Edward.

Everyone except Poppy thought this was a brilliant idea. They gathered everything they needed and went to Honey's, leaving Poppy all on her own.

Poppy ran to the playroom. Hot tears pricked her eyes.

"What's the matter?" asked Mum.

"Nobody likes me," said Poppy. "They have gone to Honey's without me, and all because of the stupid play."

"Do you really think it is just about the play," asked Mum, "or about you?"

"Maybe a bit about me," said Poppy. "I was quite bossy, but only because I wanted everything to be perfect. I still want to be in the play but I don't think they will let me. What am I going to do?"

"What do you think you should do?" asked Mum.

"Say sorry," said Poppy.

"What if no one will speak to me?" thought Poppy as she walked over to Honeypot Cottage.

Poppy pushed the gate open and they all turned to look at her.

"I am really, really sorry for being so bossy and horrible and selfish. Please can I be in your play? I promise I will do what I am told," said Poppy before anyone else had a chance to say anything.

"Come on, then," said Daisy. "You can help us finish the tickets.

"Thank you!" said Poppy.

When the tickets were done they picked up everything they needed for the play and went back to Poppy's garden.

"Perfect timing!" said Grandpa. "I have just finished the story."

"What is it called?" asked Honey.

"*Princess Bossy Boots!*" said Grandpa. Everyone laughed, even Poppy.

"And who am I?" asked Edward.

"The wizard, of course," said Grandpa. "And Mum is going to be the Fairy Godmother."

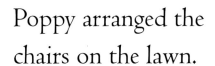

Poppy arranged the
chairs on the lawn.

Honey set off round
the village to deliver
the tickets.

Daisy got the
costumes ready.

And Edward finished
clearing the garden.

After a dress rehearsal, they were ready.

The audience started arriving. They took their seats and waited for the play to begin.

Daisy, Poppy and Honey came onto the 'stage' and Grandpa told the story.

One day Princess Poppy and Princess Honey Blossom were having tea with their mother, Queen Daisy. Everything was peaceful and they were happy. Then suddenly, there was an icy chill in the air. The wicked wizard had returned!

Edward swept onto the 'stage'.

"Ha-ha!" he cackled as he threw magic bossy dust at the princesses. "You won't be perfect now!"

The dust missed Honey Blossom, but Poppy was covered. From that moment on, Poppy was the most horrid, bossy and selfish princess ever. Everyone called her Princess Bossy Boots.

The Queen and Honey Blossom missed the old Poppy. They searched far and wide for someone to break the spell. A year went by, then, just as they were about to give up hope, Poppy's Fairy Godmother appeared!

Mum fluttered onto the 'stage', wearing
a silver dress and fairy wings. She
sprinkled a magical potion over
Poppy and waved her wand.

"Goodbye, Princess Bossy Boots!" she said.

At last, the old Poppy was back! Poppy, Honey Blossom and Queen Daisy locked the wicked wizard in the tower, threw away the key and lived happily ever after.

The audience clapped
and cheered. Poppy,
Honey, Daisy, Edward,
Grandpa and Mum
held hands and took
a bow. What a great
team they were.

"I loved being a princess in the play," said Poppy. "I wish I could be a princess all the time."

"You can only be a princess if you're not bossy and selfish, and you know what you're like!" joked Edward.

They all laughed, even Poppy. But she had learned her lesson that day. She promised herself that she would be nicer to her friends and family and not quite so bossy.